THIN ICE

Jerrold Beim

pictures by LOUIS DARLING

WILLIAM MORROW AND COMPANY
NEW YORK   1956

Lee and his brother Bobby went to school in the morning. Bobby was in the kindergarten and Lee was in the second grade. Lee liked everything about school except—

reading! Every day his teacher, Miss Hill, called a circle of children to read.

A girl named Betty read first. "A mother bird, a father bird, and two baby birds were in the nest." Betty read two pages; then it was Ned's turn. Lee knew it would be his turn next. He was scared.

"Our baby birds need something to eat," Ned began.

"Very good, Ned," Miss Hill said, when he had finished. "Now you read, Lee."

"Peep—peep—" Lee knew that word. "S—s—" He couldn't make out the next word. He was so upset that the letters seemed to dance on the page. Ned began to laugh.

Lee felt bad, but he tried not to let Ned know it.

"No laughing, please," Miss Hill said. "The word is *said*," she told Lee.

"Said the b—b—" Lee didn't know the next word, either. He was afraid that he would be laughed at again.

"Birds—" Miss Hill helped him.

How glad Lee was when his turn to read was over!

That afternoon Mother called for Bobby and Lee at school. "Why doesn't Lee read better?" Mother asked Miss Hill.

"Some boys and girls learn slowly and some fast," Miss Hill said. "I'm sure Lee really can read better than he thinks he can. He gets scared and thinks he doesn't know the words."

Lee was glad when Saturday came. There was no school, and he wouldn't have to think about reading. He went riding on his sled all morning.

After lunch Mother took Bobby and Lee to the barber shop for haircuts. Then they went to a drugstore.

"Hot chocolate?" asked Mother.

"No, ice cream," Lee said. "What kind do they have?"

"See that sign that says ice cream?" Mother said. "It tells you all the flavors."

Lee tried to read the names of the flavors, but he couldn't make out the words. Finally his mother read them to him. He had chocolate and Bobby had strawberry.

That night Dad tucked Bobby into bed first.

"Read me a story!" Bobby said.

Dad read a book about a funny king, and Lee listened too.

"This word is *king*," Dad said.
"Can you find it again?" he asked
Lee.

"I don't want to," Lee said. "I
just want to hear the story."

"I'll find it," Bobby said. "There
it is! And there! King! King! I
can read better than Lee!"

How Lee hated going to school on Monday morning! He had to read again. He didn't do very well. Ned snickered every time Lee missed a word.

"You're a dope!" Ned whispered when the children returned to their desks. "You're the worst reader in the class!"

"I don't care!" Lee said. "I don't care if I ever read at all!"

At last it was Saturday again. It was clear and cold outside.

"The pond is frozen," Mother said. "You boys can go ice skating."

Both Lee and Bobby were good skaters. They ran down the road to Walker's Pond.

They were the first ones at the pond. They put on their skates and started out over the ice. What fun it was, skimming along! Near the center of the pond, they came to a sign.

"What does it say?" Bobby asked.

"Who cares!" Lee said. It was Saturday, and he didn't have to read.

"You can't read it!" Bobby laughed. "Ned said you were the worst reader in the class!"

"I—I am not!" Lee was so mad he didn't move. He just stood there looking at the sign. That first word—anybody would know that. It looked like *peep*. But no— it began with a *K*—like *king*.

"K—eep!" he said out loud. "Keep!"

The next word he had once had in school. "Off—"

"Th—th—" he began on the next line. Was the word *the*? But the end of it was *in*. "Th—in!" he said. "Thin!"

And the last word? He had seen it somewhere. Yes—in the drugstore the day they had ice cream with Mother. Ice cream! No, just Ice.

"Ice! Keep Off, Thin Ice!" He read the whole sign aloud.

"I can read it!" he said. "It says
Keep Off, Thin Ice! Bobby—" He
turned around. Where was Bobby?
Then he saw him. He was skating
out onto the thin ice.

"Bobby! Come back! Don't skate out there!"

Bobby heard him and came a little nearer. "What do you want?" he called.

"It says Keep Off, Thin Ice!" Lee shouted. "Come back!"

"You can't read. You're making it up." Bobby laughed again and skated off.

Lee waited just a second, and then he went out after his brother.

Lee could skate faster than Bobby. He got nearer and nearer. He reached out and grabbed Bobby by the arm.

"I did read it! It says Keep Off. Come back—" Suddenly the ice beneath them felt shaky.

The ice was cracking! Bobby was scared. He held onto Lee's jacket and followed him back. The ice kept on cracking, but they finally made it to the strong ice near the shore.

"Wow! It's a good thing you made me come back!" Bobby said. "But how did you read the sign?"

"I just tried hard—and I did!" Lee exclaimed.

Other boys and girls came along.
Ned was with them.

"There's a sign out there that says Keep Off, Thin Ice," Bobby told them.

"How do you know?" Ned asked. "You can't read."

"My brother read it and he came
out and pulled me away just in
time. If it wasn't for Lee I might
have drowned!"

Bobby told his mother and father about it when he got home.

He told the boys and girls at school on Monday.

Everyone talked about how Lee had saved his brother because he could read the sign.

That morning Miss Hill called the reading circle again.

"It was very still in the house." Betty read some of the story.

Ned read too, and then it was Lee's turn. This time he wasn't so scared. He knew he could do better if he really tried. He began to read.

"'I know what they are,' said the little girl. 'They're—'" Lee looked hard at the next word.

The word looked like ice, but it had another letter in front of it.

"M—mice!" he read.

"That's right!" Miss Hill nodded.

The next word was a new one. Miss Hill had told it to the class at the start of the lesson.

"Cheese!" Lee remembered it. "Cheese is what they like," he read.

"You're getting better and better all the time!" Miss Hill said, when he finished reading. "Keep working like this, Lee, and you'll soon be a good reader!"

JERROLD BEIM was born in Newark, New Jersey, where he spent his grade-school days. "In the fourth grade of grammar school I resolved to become a writer," he says, "because of encouragement I received from my teacher who liked my theme, 'The Autobiography of a Christmas Seal.'" He attended New York University, then worked in various department stores writing advertising copy. When he sold his first story for adults to *Vanity Fair* he decided he would try to make his living as a writer, and left his department-store job. Since then he has written many books for children, including eighteen titles published by William Morrow and Company. These "short poignant stories of young modern life"* have made him one of the most popular authors writing for younger readers today.

Mr. Beim's earlier books published by Morrow include: *Laugh and Cry, The Boy on Lincoln's Lap, Country School, Mister Boss, Shoeshine Boy,* and *Country Garage.*

* From *Junior Reviewers*